Dedication

To my beautiful girlfriend, Olya,
who gave me the belief to believe.

About the Author

A. J. Brown spent fourteen adventurous years in Her Majesty's Forces as a proud member of the Royal Green Jackets, serving on operational tours across Northern Ireland, Bosnia, and Kosovo. In between the boots, the barracks, and the occasional bout of boredom, he discovered the perfect escape: books. The worlds of Douglas Adams and Terry Pratchett became firm favourites—largely because they made perfect sense of an otherwise nonsensical universe.

After hanging up his beret and embracing civilian life, A. J. found himself on new frontlines: bedtime stories. Reading How to Train Your Dragon and A Series of Unfortunate Events to his children rekindled an old dream—one involving peculiar creatures, magical mayhem, and just the right amount of narrative nonsense.

Now, with pen in hand and tongue firmly in cheek, he invites you into the whimsical, wondrous (and sometimes suspiciously well-organised) world of The Cogletts—a place where time bends, clockwork creatures scuttle, and absolutely no one is allowed to be boring.

He sincerely hopes you enjoy the journey—and that you always remember to check under your bed for rogue pocket watches.

Prologue: A Small Tick Out of Place

Time, as it turns out, is not nearly as tidy as humans like to think.

You can wear it on your wrist, hang it on the wall, or ignore it entirely until your toast catches fire. But somewhere behind all the ticking and tocking, between the seconds and the sighs, Time is being kept in order by someone far smaller—and far stranger—than you might expect.

They are called Cogletts, and they are not elves, gremlins, fairies, or dust. (Though they have been mistaken for all of those and once, quite alarmingly, for a lint bunny.)

They live inside clocks—grandfather clocks, station clocks, sundials with secrets, and occasionally even in the rattling guts of alarm clocks that haven't rung properly in years. Their job? To keep Time running smoothly. To oil the moments, polish the minutes, and give the hours a good stern talking-to when they wander off.

And among these Cogletts, none were more curious, more courageous—or more chaotic—than three small, unlikely heroes.

Dialel, who was bold and brave and often dangled from ropes at quite unreasonable heights.

Hairspring, who was precise, brilliant, and usually had a plan (or three) before Dialel finished falling.

And Geartrain, whose thoughts wandered like unguarded socks in a breeze, but who always managed to be exactly where he needed to be—even if he didn't know why.

For centuries, the great clocks ticked on. Time was kept. Secrets were safe. The past remained where it should be, and the future stayed politely in the queue.

But one day, at Shepton Gate Clock, something very peculiar happened.

A hand went missing.

Not a human hand. (That would be messy.) A *clock* hand. And not just any hand—one of *the* Hands of Time.

You see, Time—real Time—isn't just numbers and gears and old men with beards. It's something ancient. Something powerful. Something that can, if mishandled, shatter the entire world into yesterdays that never were.

So when that hand vanished, the clocks shivered.

When another followed, the gears began to whisper.

And when three small Cogletts were accused of a crime they did not commit...

Time. Started. To. Run.

Backwards.

Or forwards.

Or possibly sideways.

But don't worry. Because this is where the story begins. And if you're reading this, then there's still Time left to put everything right.

(Probably.)

CHAPTER 1: You Are Now Leaving Ben

It was a cold, early December morning; the sun had just started to yawn and stretch over the tall buildings and houses of the city of London. A low mist rolled lazily over the Thames, high enough that the stone walls lining the banks were hidden beneath it. The traffic crossing the bridges appeared to float mid-air—like an optical illusion performed by tired infrastructure and too much fog.

Just as the unmistakable sight of a red double-decker bus trundled over Westminster Bridge, the hourly chimes of Big Ben began to mark the time—7:00 a.m., loud and proud. People rushed along the pavements with the kind of urgency only Londoners can muster before coffee. Shop shutters clattered open. Newspapers slapped onto stands. Life was beginning exactly as it did every other day in London: chaotically punctual.

High above the streets and far above the mist, basking in the golden glow of the awakening sun, the four majestic faces of Big Ben gleamed quietly. You could hear the mechanical symphony of cogs and chains and levers moving the hands into place. It all seemed to happen on its own—just machines doing machiney things. But, as with most things in London, what you see is only half the truth.

Behind those iconic clock faces, nestled amongst turning cogs and chattering chains, is one of the smallest, busiest cities in London. And completely invisible to all humans—unless, of course, you happen to be magic or from the more obscure corners of myth. For behind the workings of this mighty clock live hundreds of Cogletts.

Today was especially important for three of them, as they were about to be sent upriver to the Royal Observatory in Greenwich to work on the much smaller but oh-so-crucial 24-hour clock. This isn't just any clock. This clock controls time all over the world. It even powers the magical mechanism inside Santa's sleigh, the one that lets him deliver presents across the entire globe in a single night. Nobody really knows where that power comes from—some say it's elf dust, others whisper about reindeer flatulence—but one thing's for certain: the only other clock with such mysterious energy doesn't even have hands.

That clock... is Stonehenge.

Meanwhile, just below the roman numeral VII on Big Ben's face, a loud banging and crashing erupted. It sounded remarkably like someone throwing pots and pans around a kitchen in a temper, which was not far off. Dialel had overslept.

This was a rare offence for a Coglett—but not for Dialel. He was, as the others politely put it, *unusual*. Raised on a Cornish surfer's wristwatch, Dialel had grown up with a laid-back, sea-salty attitude that did not gel well with the ticking, tocking hustle of the big city. He had never truly adjusted to London life and frankly, had no intention of trying. Geartrain—his best friend and complete opposite—was undoubtedly on his way to collect him, no doubt furious and punctual as ever.

"Dialel, hurry up! We will be late!" shouted Geartrain as he burst into the room.

Seeing Dialel not even half ready, he let out a groan that started in his boots and rumbled up through his eyebrows.

"I'm nearly ready, chill out will you," said Dialel, flipping a piece of pigeon egg toast in a pan. It was his favourite breakfast (though one must admit, if you lived in clocks, pigeons were a common sight and their eggs even more so).

Both wore black dungarees over white shirts—the official uniform of Cogletts, designed to blend into the monochrome faces of clocks. Geartrain marched over, snatched the pan, and flung it aside. The toast flew out of the window, spiralling gracefully through the morning air until it landed—splat!—squarely on the shoulder of a policeman standing below.

"Urggh!" the officer exclaimed, staring at the white goo now decorating his uniform.

"Why did you do that?" Dialel gasped. "I was *just* about to eat that!"

"We haven't got time," Geartrain said through gritted teeth, now gripping his friend by both arms. "We've got to meet Hairspring at the travel junction in five parri."

(*A parri*, for the uninitiated, is Coglett time. For every minute that passes for humans, sixty parri tick by for the Cogletts. Which might explain why they're usually so quick—unless you're Dialel.)

"You're always making us late," Geartrain huffed.

"Relax, we'll be fine," Dialel said, utterly unbothered, pulling on his boots one at a time. "We can jump on the Crown Wheel and still get there with time to spare."

"Honestly, we'll never get to stay in Greenwich if you keep this up!" Geartrain's voice was climbing the octaves now. He was a stickler for timekeeping—he came from a long line of clocksmiths, with ancestors who'd polished the very first pocket watch carried by the first royal guard to parade outside Buckingham Palace. It baffled him why he remained best friends with someone as tardy and chaotic as Dialel.

But Dialel, while frustratingly laid back, was also daring thrill seeker with a heart as loyal as a spring-loaded latch. Where Geartrain hesitated (especially with heights, which was unfortunate given their job description), Dialel leapt. It was largely thanks to him that the clock face stayed clean, the hands remained polished, and no one had plummeted to their doom in two years.

Now ready, the two of them dashed out and sprinted towards the sign marked *Crown Wheel*.

"I really don't know what you worry about," panted Dialel. "Look—no one else is heading this way."

Naturally, they turned the corner and were confronted by a three-Cogletts-deep crowd, all waiting for the Crown Wheel to take them to other sectors of the clock. (If you've ever tried to board the Jubilee Line at 8 a.m., you'll have an idea.)

"You were saying?" muttered Geartrain.

Dialel whipped a rope from around his shoulder. At the end? A grappling hook.

"Hold on!"

Before Geartrain could object, the hook flew upwards, caught onto a smaller moving escapement wheel, and hoisted them both high above the crowd. They spun leftward, twirling midair like circus performers.

Geartrain screamed.

He hated it when Dialel did this.

Dialel yanked the rope, dislodged the hook, and they plummeted down—landing in a heap at the front of the queue on the edge of the Crown Wheel.

"See? No one's going *this* way," Dialel grinned.

Geartrain was pale, mildly traumatised, and possibly missing a filling. But even he let out a little giggle.

They still had plenty of time. The Crown Wheel spun smoothly, carrying them around the inner workings of Big Ben like a theme park ride for extremely small engineers. Within a quarter of a parri, they'd arrived at Travel Junction.

Standing on the corner, adjusting the strap of her satchel with the precision of someone who could recalibrate a pendulum blindfolded, was **Hairspring**.

She had never left Big Ben. Not once. She had memorised every tooth of its gears, every tick of its temperamental chime, and once rewired an entire escapement mechanism using a discarded paperclip and sheer determination. While she dreamed of travel, Hairspring also liked structure, order, and plans with labelled diagrams. She believed in facts, figures, and finishing your maintenance logs *on time*.

But that didn't mean she was afraid.

No, Hairspring wasn't the sort to tremble when a clock skipped a beat or when Time itself started fraying at the edges. She faced problems the way she faced a jammed minute wheel: with grit, logic, and the occasional use of a sharply worded glare.

She had worked with Geartrain and Dialel for years now—mostly keeping them from being squashed, scorched, or permanently ejected from various timepieces. And though she would never admit it aloud (unless under extreme duress or perhaps bribed with tea), she had grown rather fond of them—especially the chaotic one with the scruffy hair and the chronic inability to arrive anywhere on schedule.

They needed her.

And secretly, though she would've rather wrestled a rusted cog than admit it...

She needed them too.

Travel Junction, to human eyes, might've resembled a mix between an airport, a train station, and a potting shed. It was nestled on the north-facing side of Big Ben, tucked behind the numeral X, with three departure platforms:

- **Platform 1: GLOBAL** (Clocks of international repute—Time Square, Tokyo Station, the Pizza Hut clock in downtown Chicago that runs five minutes fast).

- **Platform 2: OFT: OFFICIALS ONLY** (This was how you reached Old Father Time. It was written in big bold letters and guarded by two Cogletts who looked like they bench-pressed springs for fun).

- **Platform 3: ANGLELAND, ANGLELAND** (A naming accident. One Coglett once lived inside the Wembley stadium scoreboard, and after hearing the humans chant "Eng-er-land," misunderstood the pronunciation. It stuck.)

Dialel and Geartrain stepped into the concourse, scanning for Hairspring.

She spotted them first, waved and jogged over.

"Hey, you two. I didn't think you were going to make it," she beamed, giving Dialel a meaningful look. She *knew* it was his fault, but they were here, and that was all that mattered.

Geartrain pointed at Dialel, mouthing, *You already know why.*

Dialel just gave her a cheeky grin.

Platform 3 was heaving. Cogletts bustled about in various uniforms—beachwear for coastal clocks, suits for the more formal posts like the Bank of England. All wore black and white, blending with clock faces like living camouflage.

Unlike humans, Cogletts didn't board trains. Each platform held rows of blooming dandelions (yes, those cheerful yellow weeds). Every three parri, the petals turned white and puffy, transforming into tiny parachutes. Cogletts, being natural time-travelling tinkerers, had learned to harness these seeds—controlling their direction, destination, and speed.

At the back of the room stood a pair of enormous bellows.

When the time was right, they'd blow the seeds—and the passengers—out into the world.

The three friends stood before a flower, waiting for it to shift from yellow to white.

Dialel was bouncing with excitement. Hairspring could barely contain her own.

Geartrain looked like he might faint.

The petals changed. The bellows inhaled.

WHOOSH.

Three tiny shapes launched into the sky, arcing out of Big Ben, banking right over the misty river below toward Greenwich.

And the only sound left behind was the faint, high-pitched scream of a very unhappy Geartrain.

CHAPTER 2: Greenwich MEAN Time

For a human, it would take approximately forty-two minutes to travel from Embankment to Greenwich by boat—assuming the tide, the tourists, and the Thames all agreed to cooperate. But Coglett time is a different kettle of springs entirely. It zips along faster than a squirrel on espresso and doesn't care much for timetables or nautical charts.

Hairspring could hardly contain herself. She hooped and hollered with pure glee as the three Cogletts zipped past the Tower of London, swooshed over Tower Bridge, and zoomed by that very tall glass toothpick the humans call the Shard. She shouted and pointed excitedly at everything like a tourist on their first hovercar ride, trying to catch Dialel's and Geartrain's attention.

Suddenly, a seagull—clearly having a bad feather day—swooped down from above. The draft it created caught Hairspring's seed, tugging it downward toward the river.

Dialel's eyes widened. With a swift motion, he grabbed one of the trailing strands of his own seed, yanked hard, and veered downward. He descended like a heroic leaf in a hurricane.

"Quickly! Push up on the strands—QUICK!" he yelled.

Hairspring gripped her seed and shoved upwards with all her strength, just as her toes skimmed the Thames. The seed rose again, wobbling slightly.

"That was a close one," Dialel shouted, hovering beside her. "Haven't you had your seed flight lessons?"

Hairspring scowled, cheeks flushed. "*Of course* I have! I just haven't been outside the simulator before."

By now, they'd caught up to Geartrain, who hadn't noticed a thing—his eyes had been glued shut the entire time. He opened one cautiously to peek.

"Where have you two been?" he asked, blinking at the sudden brightness. "Look, that's the Old Naval College. We're nearly there."

The seeds began their descent toward Shepards Gate and the famous Prime Meridian Line. The early morning sun had begun to stretch lazily into the sky, its golden beams slicing through the leafless branches like butter through toast. The clock face below gleamed, bathed in morning light.

"So many numbers," Dialel groaned, squinting. "Double the cleaning."

"Aim for the left of the clock, where the IX should be!" Hairspring shouted, correcting her course.

"Where?!" Geartrain yelled back, eyes now flitting wildly across the dial.

"There! The XVIII!" she pointed.

Just then, a small door popped open beside the clock's rim. Glowing green arrows pointed inside like helpful but impatient exit signs.

With a whoosh, the three Cogletts zipped straight into the clock, landing smoothly onto a platform beneath a grand sign:

YOU HAVE ARRIVED AT THE CENTRE OF TIME

As they climbed down from their now-shedding seed parachutes, they stood in awe. Around them were Cogletts from all corners of the globe—Swiss ones, who looked very precise; French ones, who looked very unimpressed; and even one wearing a poncho who seemed mildly lost.

Already the seeds were changing again, petals turning yellow and curling delicately into dandelions once more.

Standing by the exit were two rather severe-looking Cogletts. The taller of the pair was dressed in a smart black uniform so stiff it could probably walk on its own. His name was Akea, and he hailed from the island nation of Vizibaltia, somewhere deep in the middle of the Pacific Ocean (and largely unknown to both humans and reasonably up-to-date atlases).

Akea hated Greenwich. He hated the sign. He hated London in general, and he muttered "*Centre of Time*" under his breath with such venom it could curdle milk. In his own language, "Akea" meant *nothing*. Ironically, "nothing" was also used as *zero*, which led many of his less respectful colleagues to call him "Zero" behind his back. This did not help his sunny disposition.

Next to him stood Tetia—a skinny, angular Coglett with the nervous twitch of someone who drank too much cog grease. Akea elbowed him sharply and pointed to a rope hanging on the wall. Tetia yanked it. A large screen whirred down from the ceiling with a hum that sounded suspiciously smug. Words flashed across it in golden letters:

"NEW INTAKE: MOVE DIRECTLY TO INSPECTION – FIFTH FLOOR."

Hairspring spotted the sign and seized Dialel and Geartrain by the arms.

"Old Father Time!" groaned Geartrain. "Steady on, there's no rush, you know!"

"Let's go, let's go!" she beamed, dragging them toward the door like a child heading into a sweet shop.

As they passed the two guards, Akea whispered something to Tetia. Dialel glanced back, puzzled.

In front of them now were the elevators: long vertical chains with open ledges, each surrounded by a modest fence that was more suggestion than protection. Cogletts queued politely for the chain marked *Floor 5*. The trio climbed aboard with a handful of others, and the lift shot upwards like an enthusiastic yo-yo.

They peered out over the workings of the Greenwich clock.

"Isn't it… small?" Hairspring said, eyes wide.

"What were you expecting?" Dialel asked with mock grandeur. "A palace?"

"I don't know," she replied, bashfully. "I've only ever seen Big Ben. This is *the* world clock! I just… thought it'd be bigger."

They arrived on the fifth floor and stepped into a large open room. Painted on the floor were eight numbered boxes.

Akea and Tetia stormed in like thunderclouds in jackboots.

"ATTENTION! Stand in a box—in groups of three!" Tetia barked.

Cogletts scattered like startled crumbs. Hairspring dragged Dialel and Geartrain into Box 3.

"YOU THERE!" Akea barked. "Not that one. Box 8!"

They looked at each other, collectively baffled, but moved obediently to the final box.

Akea stepped onto a podium bearing a carved hourglass. He surveyed the new recruits like a disapproving librarian.

"Welcome to Shepards Gate," he sneered. "You are supposedly the best your countries have to offer." His tone suggested he thought otherwise.

"You all look like a complete waste of my parri, but alas—here you are."

Tetia scanned the crowd with a grin that could melt cheese—and not in a good way.

"You will be given jobs. You will be given uniforms. You will be allocated living quarters," Akea continued. "First: inspection. Let's see what we're working with."

What followed was a masterclass in military poking, scowling, and item-tossing. Akea and Tetia worked down the line, shouting at hats, shoes, and hairstyles alike.

Finally, they arrived at Box 8.

"So, you're all from Big Ben?" Akea asked, his nose wrinkling.

They nodded.

"ANSWER THE COMMANDER!" Tetia bellowed.

"Yes!" the trio chorused in unison.

Akea jabbed a finger into Dialel's chest.

"What sort of haircut is *that*?"

Dialel blinked.

"And what's that rope for?"

Dialel opened his mouth, but Akea had already moved on to stare down Geartrain.

"Why are you shaking? What's wrong with you?"

Geartrain tried to answer, but Tetia pushed him aside to reach Hairspring.

Still giddy to be there, she grinned brightly.

"DO NOT SMILE AT ME!" Akea roared, nose practically touching hers. "Who and where do you think you *are*?!"

Her smile vanished.

"You're scum. Lazy. City dwellers. I don't want you here, I don't like you, and I certainly don't like *COGS* from Landan!"

He practically spat the last word.

"But... you're here now. So: sunrise cleaning duty. Face of the clock. Report to the door next to the II. Don't be late."

And with that, the inspection was over.

Murmurs of discontent rippled through the other groups. Dialel turned to his friends and muttered, "What an absolute broken dial cap."

(*Translation: The worst insult a Coglett can offer. Not printable in polite horology.*)

Tetia marched off, leading them down a long, dim corridor. Every so often, other groups were ushered into tidy dormitories. But not this group.

Oh no.

They were led further and further from the clock face until they reached a door so ancient it had cobwebs older than most time zones. Tetia shoved it open with his shoulder.

The room reeked of dust, stale air, and mild resentment.

"This is your room. Inspections are every Friday at 1900 hours. It better be immaculate, or there will be *trouble*."

Hairspring smiled hopefully.

Geartrain stood to attention.

Dialel groaned. "Friday at 1900?! That's less than fifteen parri away…"

Tetia's footsteps echoed off into the distance.

The room itself resembled a rejected storeroom. Three beds—two on their headboards and one propped sadly against a wall. A wardrobe missing half its doors. Cobwebs big enough to have their own postcodes.

Inside the wardrobe, they found three uniforms… or rather, the *ghosts* of uniforms. Faded to a sorry grey, they looked like even moths had turned them down.

Hairspring, determined not to be defeated, seized a broom and began sweeping. Dialel and Geartrain righted the beds and positioned the wardrobe to give Hairspring some privacy.

After ten parri of frantic work, the place almost resembled a room fit for living.

Then the door burst open.

"INSPECTION TIME. STAND BY YOUR BEDS!"

"But… but it's not 1900!" Geartrain objected, horrified.

Akea smirked.

"You're in *my* time now."

What followed was carnage.

Beds flipped. Wardrobe kicked over. Uniforms hurled into the hallway.

"Well, your first inspection didn't go so well, now did it?" Akea sneered.

"Sunrise tomorrow. Clock face entrance—door by the II. *Don't* be late."

With matching grins, Akea and Tetia swaggered off.

For the first time since leaving Big Ben, Hairspring wasn't smiling.

Geartrain sat heavily on the nearest upright piece of furniture, muttering about procedural violations.

Dialel scratched his head, then grinned.

"Well, I think it's quite obvious—they *really* like us. Chin up. Let's get the room back in order and get some sleep. I've got a feeling tomorrow's going to be a busy day."

CHAPTER 3: What Is the Time and Who Are You?

Eight human days had passed.

Life had not, in any meaningful way, improved for our three clock-bound adventurers. If it wasn't Akea assigning them the most soul-sapping, tick-polishing tasks in the building, it was Tetia ripping apart their room with the kind of glee normally reserved for toddlers and demolition crews.

Dialel's usual happy-go-lucky spirit was beginning to wear thinner than a cheap mainspring, and Hairspring had taken to staring wistfully out of the clockface at every opportunity, eyes scanning the skyline for a glimpse of Big Ben. She and Geartrain had grown so homesick that their conversations now mostly consisted of nostalgic arguments over which side of Big Ben had the better view.

Outside, the world trudged on unaware. It was a thoroughly Decemberish day in Greenwich Park. Rain was falling at just the right angle to ensure maximum sock saturation, puddles had gathered conspiratorially along the paths, and the sky had taken on that familiar grey-soup colour reserved only for British winter. And yet, despite the gloom, the humans seemed... happy.

It was the 20th of December. Nearly Christmas. Hope, inexplicably, was winning.

Inside the clock, however, three Cogletts were trudging toward the face once more for yet another 3600 parri of cleaning. That's one full rotation of a minute hand—though it *feels* much longer when you're scrubbing brass with only pigeon spit and elbow grease.

They reached the small door beside the number II. Dialel was tying the rope around his waist with his usual dramatic flair, preparing to swing outside. That was when he noticed something odd.

Akea was approaching.

And for once, he looked... rattled.

His immaculate uniform was slightly crumpled. His hat was on at a non-regulation tilt. His boots had scuff marks. *Scuff marks*, on Akea.

"Something wrong?" asked Dialel with a smirk that could polish glass.

"No. Nothing wrong. Just get on with your work," Akea snapped, unusually curt.

Geartrain had just opened the door when something green and glinty caught Hairspring's eye—something slipping from inside Akea's jacket. Before anyone could comment, Akea shoved past them, knocking Dialel off balance just as he threw his hook out the door.

With a yelp and a wildly flailing arm, Dialel tumbled forward.

Fortunately, the grappling hook caught one of the clockface numerals—specifically the rather smugly positioned IIII—and the rope snapped taut just before Dialel could become a very unfortunate stain at the bottom of the clock case.

Dangling in midair, heart pounding, Dialel looked up to see… no one looking back.

His friends weren't even watching.

They were staring *through* the glass.

On the other side, outside in the drizzling park, stood an old man.

He was watching them.

And then—more unsettling still—he looked directly at *Dialel*.

Now, this should not have been possible. Humans *cannot* see Cogletts. It's a rule. A big one. Right up there with "never wind a cuckoo backwards" and "never drink second-hand tea."

The man was dressed impeccably in a tan tweed suit, a dark blue cravat pinned with three shimmering crystals, and a wide-brimmed hat that would've made a scarecrow weep with envy. He carried a shiny black cane topped with a crystal so large it might've once belonged in a chandelier.

He opened his mouth as if to speak... then paused. Slowly, he raised his cane and tapped the glass of the clock three times.

Tap. Tap. Tap.

On the third tap, the crystal on the cane glowed—then flashed.

In a blink of white light and the peculiar smell of static and cinnamon, Dialel, Geartrain, and Hairspring were no longer inside the clock.

They were standing beside the old man, in the park, staring *at* the clock.

Dazed, disoriented, and suspiciously damp, they noticed something else.

Everyone around them was moving in slow motion, like molasses in December. But it didn't last long. Time snapped back into place with a jolt—and so did their new height.

They were all roughly 5 feet 6 inches tall.

"Don't worry," the old man said in a voice that sounded like it came with its own echo. "It will pass. You're coming out of *parri* time and into the human world."

"What?!" they all blurted at once.

"Who?!"

"How?!"

"Why?!"

"WHAT?!" Dialel finished, arms flailing.

The old man didn't seem fazed.

"What time is it?" he asked, calmly.

"Its…" Geartrain began, looking at the clock.

He paused.

"It is…" Hairspring tried to continue, but faltered too.

Dialel squinted up at the clock. "Wait… where are the hands?"

"Exactly," said the man, with a nod.

Dialel's stomach did a slow somersault. He realised that when he fell, he hadn't hit the hands at all—because they weren't there. But he'd been too busy not plummeting to his doom to notice.

"But… you saw us. Humans can't see us. Can they? Is it the glass? Or the cane? *What's going on?*"

"Come with me," the man said, suddenly whispering. "I'll explain what I think might be happening."

Still baffled, bewildered, and about three shoe sizes too tall, the three friends followed him to a nearby park shelter—a creaky wooden gazebo with a view of the clock tower and the atmosphere of an old biscuit tin.

"Who *are* you?" Dialel demanded, hands on his hips.

"I've known you your entire lives," the man said simply. "In fact, I was hoping I'd meet you today."

The three stared.

"But… you're human?" Hairspring asked hesitantly.

"Am I?" he replied with a mischievous grin.

"Oh, enough!" snapped Geartrain, arms flailing in frustration. "I *cannot* take any more riddles!"

"Fine, fine," the man said, lifting his hands. "Many know me as Old Father Time. You Cogletts tend to shorten it to OFT."

Had they not been enchanted, the three would've needed to gather their jaws from the floor.

OFT tapped his cane on the wet paving stones.

There was a spark.

A flash.

And a *pouf* of smoke—so white it made snow feel self-conscious.

When the smoke cleared, the old man had changed.

Now he stood taller, with long flowing black hair, bright blue eyes, and a neatly plaited beard. His tweed suit had transformed into a tan-brown smock with and a very long scarf that looked like it had been knitted by someone with infinite yarn and no social plans. The hat remained—he was quite fond of it, as he thought it made him look younger—and the cane had morphed into a gleaming staff tipped with swirling light.

He looked like a wizard who had walked straight off the cover of a fantasy novel and accidentally wandered into a timepiece museum.

"Old Father Time…" Geartrain whispered, reverently.

"Yes?" OFT responded innocently.

Hairspring and Dialel snorted with laughter.

"What?" OFT asked, perplexed.

"It's just..." Dialel grinned, "it's something we say. Like... surprise. You know. *Old Father Time!*"

"Oh," said OFT, mildly offended. "I see."

He looked at the three of them with eyes that held centuries.

"There's much to explain, and not a lot of time—if what I suspect is happening is, indeed, happening. You must come with me to the Master Clock."

"*Master Clock?*" the three friends echoed.

And thus, the wheels of time (and plot) began to turn.

CHAPTER 4: The Master Clock

Standing under the shelter of the park gazebo, the three friends were a muddle of confusion, damp socks, and existential questions. They looked at each other, then back at Old Father Time, who stood calmly beside them as though none of this was particularly surprising. It had, after all, been a very strange day—and it wasn't even elevenses yet.

Where were they supposed to go? What had happened to the hands of the clock? How did OFT know them? And, most importantly, what in the cogs was *The Master Clock*?

OFT turned to his right as if responding to a question only he could hear. "That one will do."

He strode toward a nearby puddle and, without any explanation or apology to the laws of physics, plunged the end of his staff into its centre. He stirred it anti-clockwise, faster and faster until the puddle began to spin—like a whirlpool in a teacup.

Dialel peered into the swirling water and saw, impossibly, green open fields spinning far below.

"What is *that*?" he muttered, eyebrows performing an acrobatic routine of their own.

"That," said OFT, pointing with grand authority, "is where we are going. Now—JUMP!"

Hairspring gave him a look reserved for people who talk to bread.

"You want us to jump into a *puddle*?" she asked, incredulous.

Geartrain folded his arms, deeply offended. "I haven't got my Wellingtons. I'll get wet feet."

"What have we got to lose?" said Dialel, grinning—and jumped without hesitation.

With a sigh and a shrug, Hairspring followed. They vanished into the whirlpool.

"JUMP!" OFT barked, grabbing Geartrain's jacket. The two of them tumbled forward just as the whirlpool began to collapse behind them.

Screaming, Geartrain landed bottom-first in what he believed to be a very small, very warm patch of mud.

"Old. Father. Time!" he shouted, horrified. "Look at me! I've landed in some—"

"I don't think that's mud," said Dialel, trying not to laugh.

Hairspring pointed discreetly at a herd of cows stampeding to the far end of the field.

"Where *are* we?" all three asked, brushing themselves off.

"Turn around," said OFT, his voice dramatic enough to deserve its own soundtrack.

They turned.

Unfortunately, a convoy of lorries chose that exact moment to roar past along the nearby A303, blocking their view entirely. As the last van trundled by, the field beyond was finally revealed—and there, rising tall and ancient in the mist, stood the monolithic stones of **Stonehenge**.

"That," said OFT with a smile, "is the Master Clock. Also, my house."

"It's a *pile of stones*," Dialel declared flatly, not even pretending to be impressed.

Hairspring elbowed him in the ribs with a glare that freeze a melted ice cube.

They crossed the road carefully—this being one of those rare interdimensional adventures where the Green Cross Code still applied—and began walking toward the ancient stones. But as they crested a small ridge, a voice called out from across the field.

"Oi! You lot—stop right there!"

A human security guard had spotted them and was now waddling their way with surprising speed and significant authority.

"Quickly, follow me!" said OFT, and broke into a run. The others scrambled after him.

As the guard shouted louder, OFT stopped beside one of the standing arches. "In here!" he commanded, gesturing between the stones. He tapped his staff once—*thud*—and vanished.

The others followed one by one, and just as Dialel slipped through, the guard reached the same spot.

"What the bejeeze just happened?" the guard muttered. His radio crackled to life with a voice asking the exact same thing.

On the other side of the stone, Dialel paused, turned back, and made a series of faces and ridiculous dances at the bewildered guard.

"Stop it," OFT hissed. "He can't see us—but let's not tempt the laws of visibility. This way."

A stone staircase appeared beneath his feet. He descended into the earth, the others following close behind. They walked for what felt like a week (or about four British cups of tea, time-wise), finally arriving at a vast underground room.

It was filled with broken cogs, cracked gears, unspooled springs, and loose screws—both literal and metaphorical.

In the centre of the room was a large, shimmering pool of liquid metal. It glowed like mercury and hummed softly, like it knew something they didn't.

"Looks like the cog indexes have detached themselves," muttered Dialel, peering at the chaos. "Bit of a state, isn't it?"

OFT, now growing fond of being addressed like a Google assistant, perched on the low stone rim of the pool.

"Sit," he said, waving a hand. "It's time I explained what I believe is... becoming evident."

"Evident?" scoffed Geartrain. "This whole situation is about as *evident* as a warm patch of questionable mud!"

"Hush, will you?" snapped Hairspring, who has finally regained her usual confidence and spark after the long days at Shepards Gate and the latest shock.

OFT plunged his staff into the pool and stirred—this time clockwise.

"I am *not* jumping in that," Geartrain began to say—

"Shut up, will you!" snapped both Dialel and Hairspring in perfect harmony.

As the liquid spun, it rose upward like a silver stalagmite, whirling faster and faster. Images shimmered inside the metal—some blurred, some glowing brightly. Reflections danced across the walls: childhood memories, unknown cities, unfamiliar faces.

Dialel swore he saw himself as a child—but not in any place he remembered.

"What... what *is* this?" he asked.

"This," OFT said solemnly, "is the history and future of the Cogletts. You are seeing what has happened—and what has not happened. Yet."

"Come again?" Dialel blinked.

"Or not," Geartrain added.

The spinning slowed. The room fell still.

And OFT began.

Theories of Time, According to Old Father Time: A Surprisingly Plausible Summary

"Humans have many theories about how time began. Some turn to science—others to myths and legends. Annoyingly, they're both kind of right."

Theory One: The Big Bang

"Millennia ago, in a forgotten corner of what is now Sagittarius A—the Milky Way's central black hole—two factions lived on a planet called *Tempus* (don't look for it; it's not there anymore).

The factions were: the Druigs and the Truids. They fought over whether to expand their planet or redecorate it.

It did not end well.

As the planet exploded—causing what humans now call the *Big Bang*—two spaceships escaped. One held the Druigs. The other, the Truids.

The Druigs' ship carried five powerful artefacts essential to controlling time itself. As they fled, their ship was struck by asteroids, The ship crash-landed on a young Earth. It buried itself deep in a glacier. This event may or may not have wiped out the dinosaurs. (It did.) The ship, was named the *Grailel*.

Theory Two: Myths and Legends

The second ship, carrying the Truids, arrived later—around 5:30 a.m., sixty-three million years ago. (No one remembers if they had coffee.)

Aboard were myself, Mother Nature, Posster Vunni (you know him as the Easter Bunny), Rolax and Tegd Heer (the original Master Clockmakers—yes, those *Rolax* and *Tegd*), and a bag of cosmic nerves.

We spread across Earth, helping early humans understand time by teaching them how to read the Sun. They didn't quite get it, so we ended up with four calendars instead of one: Lunar, Solar, Lunisolar, and the ever-confusing Pre-Modern.

Eventually, I settled here. I asked a local builder named Birticas to make me a house beneath these stones. I met a boy named Arthur King—he ran a camel showroom in Lotte. His friends were Lance, Percy, and Tristan. They became fascinated with my tales of the *Grailel* and the Druigs. They went looking… and fifteen years later, they returned—with the artefacts.

To celebrate, we made a clock using the artefacts:

- The **sword** became the clock hands.
- The **bell** an alarm.
- The **ball** for motion.
- The **metronome** for the tick-tock.
- And five crystals—quartz, naturally—as power.

We built the clock on a round-ish table made of cocoa wood. It became *The Master Clock*.

Old Father Time tapped his staff on the pool's edge. The liquid pillar collapsed, splashing a few metallic droplets onto the stone. Each one wriggled back into the pool, like guilty silver tadpoles.

Dialel stared.

"What the actual winding spring was *that*?! It doesn't explain why we're here, how you know us, or where the clock hands went!"

"I was getting to that," OFT said gently.

"Druigs are Cogletts—but not nice ones. They were frozen in the glacier after the crash, but some survived. When humans began exploring the Earth and building fires… the ice melted.

One of these Druigs found my home last night. My green quartz crystal was stolen. I followed the signal—to the clock at Greenwich.

Dialel, you're descended from Mari-Time, a Druigian who escaped on the *Grailel*. I placed you with a family in Mawgan Porth, Cornwall.

Hairspring—your parents have watched over Big Ben for decades.

And Geartrain—I've seen you marching like a soldier outside Buckingham Palace."

"Really?" Geartrain perked up. "Was I any good? I've always thought I'd look fantastic in one of those big fuzzy hats."

Hairspring rolled her eyes. OFT continued.

"Some Druigs made peace. But others… others want the artefacts back. And they want Earth to look more like Tempus. I suspect the thief not only stole my crystal—but also found where the artefacts were hidden."

"Wait… *hidden*?" said Dialel. "I thought you had them here?"

"Eight hundred years ago, another Druig broke in. After that, I hid the artefacts across the world—in plain and secret sight."

"The hands of the Shepards Gate clock," he added, "are forged from the blade of Excalibur."

"But clock hands are tiny!" Hairspring protested. "A sword would be massive!"

"Yes. The *rest* of the steel is in other clocks. And our thief... is heading for them."

He touched his staff to the mercury pool. The silver rose again, spun briefly, and then collapsed with a splash in the shape of a delicate, gleaming **crown**.

As the liquid stilled, it revealed a glowing map—and marked on it, the locations of the remaining pieces of the sword.

CHAPTER 5: I'm Not a THIEF!

While OFT and the three not-so-little-anymore Cogletts were busy trying to piece together the past, the present, and an alarming amount of future, back at Shepards Gate things were getting... suspiciously smooth.

Akea and Tetia were having a delightful time.

Their plan, as far as villainous plans go, was unfolding nicely—like an evil origami swan that flaps its wings and bites your fingers when you least expect it.

You see, Akea had not only survived the Grailel crash—he had thrived. After years of lying dormant, then less dormant, and eventually thoroughly awake, he had settled on the tiny, secretive island of Vizibaltia in the Pacific Ocean, spending centuries trying to complete what his father had started (and arguably, catastrophically failed at) on the planet Tempus.

Akea's greatest grievance? The number **zero**.

The Truids—the time-loving, calendar-wielding, Sun-chasing beings—had refused to use zero in their systems. No zero in their maths. No zero in their clocks. No zero in their Roman numerals. Just endless I's and V's and X's, which frankly looked like the worst sort of crossword puzzle.

To Akea and the Druigs, this was a *travesty*.

After all, if there's nothing to count... why not count the *nothing*?

It was this philosophical noodle-knot that had led, in part, to the destruction of their home planet. Because Akea's father had tried to squeeze a zero into the ancient time code. The system, unsurprisingly, had objected violently. The alarm that followed triggered a catastrophic chain reaction, which caused the explosion known across space and time as the Big Bang.

The irony? He hadn't been trying to destroy anything. He'd just wanted to *save* Tempus. Unfortunately, by the time the warning went out, the Grailel had already fled, carrying the youngest Druigs—Akea among them.

Frozen for several million years would make anyone a little moody. But Akea's upbringing—among the surviving Druigs—had filled him with tales of heroic sacrifice and divine purpose. In their version of history, Akea's father was a martyr, not a mathematical disaster.

Now, back at Shepards Gate, far from the ticking heart of the clock, Akea and Tetia sat in a dark, dusty storeroom plotting their next move.

"So, what is the plan then?" Tetia asked, peeling the label off a tin of polishing wax.

Akea pulled a battered brown leather book from his jacket and placed it on the table.

"I need to check something," he muttered, flipping to a dog-eared page. "We have to find all the missing artefact sections. Once we reunite them… we'll be able to—"

At that moment, a young Coglett came pelting down the corridor, face flushed and breath wheezing.

"Sir! Sir! The Timekeeper wants to see you! *The hands are missing!*" he panted.

"They're *what*?!" Akea gasped, doing a remarkable impression of a man utterly shocked.

Tetia stood bolt upright, eyes wide with pretend innocence.

Akea snatched the book off the table and shoved it into his jacket. "This is very serious," he said, his tone just the right side of sincere. "Let's go."

The Timekeeper's office, as you would expect, was a tidy, uninspired little room wedged behind the X and II of the twelve. It had a large desk, naturally red mahogany, a few bookcases, and a window overlooking the humans below—who were all staring at the clock in mild confusion.

The Timekeeper himself was a stout Coglett with wispy hair standing on end like he'd recently licked a battery. He turned to face them, cheeks redder than a tomato under pressure.

"**EXPLAIN!**" he bellowed, advancing toward Akea and Tetia like an angry sofa with legs.

"We… can't, sir," Akea replied, doing his best impression of a calm, competent subordinate.

"WHERE ARE THE HANDS?!" the Timekeeper roared. "WHERE IS THE MORNING CREW?!"

Now that *did* catch Akea off guard. He hadn't realised Dialel and the others had vanished. But his mind, as ever, was three cogs ahead.

Perfect.

This was better than he could've planned.

He feigned horror.

"They must have *stolen* them!" he blurted. "Dialel, Geartrain, and the girl—Hairspring! They were here this morning. Then *poof!* Gone. And so are the hands."

Tetia looked over at him in surprise, the dawning realisation spreading across his face like marmalade. Then he smirked.

The Timekeeper didn't need further convincing.

"FIND THEM! FIND THEM *NOW!* Send word to all clocks! They've stolen the hands!"

He paused, breathing hard. "Send it via Cuckoo carrier!"

(Ah yes—the Cuckoo Carrier. Like a pigeon post, only the mail travels through Cuckoo clocks, which ensures it's *always* on time, though sometimes delivered with an annoying chime.)

"Yes, sir!" Akea and Tetia chorused, turning sharply on their heels and marching from the office—evil grins now painted firmly across their faces.

In the Cuckoo Mailroom, the pair scribbled their message in large block capitals:

**STOP ON SIGHT: DIALEL, GEARTRAIN & HAIRSPRING.
THEY HAVE STOLEN THE HANDS OF TIME.**
(*Underlined. Twice.*)

They handed the paper to a sleepy-looking postmaster behind the counter.

"National or international?" he asked, without looking up.

"What's the difference?" Akea snapped.

"About six quid," the postmaster replied, whistling as he filed some stamps.

"You're a thief!" Tetia muttered to Akea.

"Have you *read* it?" Akea asked the postmaster.

"I don't read customers' mail. Against the rules," came the flat reply.

"READ. IT." Akea growled, teeth clenched.

The postmaster sighed, picked up the paper, and frowned. Then he bent down, pulled out a different form and slapped it on the counter.

"Sorry. Wrong paperwork. You've got to use *this* one."

Akea turned a shade of red not yet named by science.

He grabbed a pen and began angrily rewriting the message.

"You need to use *black* ink," Tetia added helpfully.

It was a miracle the mailroom didn't explode.

Once the proper form was filled in (and checked twice), it was fed into the correct machine.

Within seconds, cuckoo clocks all across England sprang into action. Tiny doors burst open, birds popped out, and a chorus of little mechanical voices echoed across the land:

"Dialel, Geartrain, and Hairspring are wanted for the theft of the Hands of Time!"

Some clocks even chimed in dramatic minor keys, just to be helpful.

The postmaster didn't look up.

"Have a nice day," he said flatly, sorting through a stack of incoming letters marked URGENT and smelling faintly of cheese.

Back in their gloomy little hideout, Akea and Tetia sat with smug satisfaction.

"This is *perfect*," Akea beamed. "They've vanished. Everyone thinks they're guilty. We can move freely now. Through clocks. Through time zones. No one will question it."

"Ohhh," Tetia said slowly, realisation dawning like a sunrise behind very thick curtains.

Akea pulled out his book again, flipping to a page marked with a curled corner.

His eyes scanned the text quickly, lips muttering. But then his expression shifted.

From smug… to unsettled.

"What is it?" Tetia asked.

"We need another crystal," Akea said, voice low. "The next location is locked. We can't reach it without it."

He rounded on Tetia.

"You were supposed to get the crystals from OFT's house!"

"I *tried!*" Tetia yelped. "The old man started to *wake up!*"

He paused, looked down.

"I'm not a *thief*," he whispered.

Akea's expression hardened.

"It's too late for that."

He slammed the book shut, storming from the room.

"Let's go."

Tetia followed, reluctant but loyal.

Behind them, the message echoed again through the clocks of the world:

**STOP ON SIGHT:
THEY HAVE STOLEN THE HANDS OF TIME.**

CHAPTER 6: It's Time for the News

Geartrain was rummaging around in OFT's kitchen.

"Have you got anything to eat?" he asked, trying to be polite while already halfway through the cupboards. "I'm a whiz in the kitchen—I could knock up some woodlouse bacon sandwiches or a pigeon omelette?"

"I think there are some wood pigeon eggs in the fridge," OFT replied, barely glancing up.

"Ooooooooh! *Wood* pigeon? Posh! All we ever get in London is sky-rat pigeon eggs," Geartrain muttered, pulling the eggs from the fridge with a chef's reverence.

At that precise moment, a very loud cuckoo clock sprang to life.

Cuckoo! CUCKOO! CUCKOO!

Startled, Geartrain launched the eggs into the air like feathery missiles. They reached an impressive height before plummeting to the ground and exploding with a dramatic squelch.

"Oh, broken watch strap…" he groaned. "I guess I'm never going to try them."

"What was *that*?" Hairspring gasped. "I've never heard the cuckoo mail that loud before."

"I have," OFT said gravely. "Once. Just before an explosion destroyed my world."

There was a beat of silence.

Protruding from the front of the cuckoo clock was a sheet of red paper. It trembled ominously, as if it knew it bore bad news.

OFT snatched it and read aloud:

"**Dialel, Hairspring, and Geartrain—wanted for the heinous crime of stealing the Shepards Gate clock hands… and failing to complete their daily cleaning duties.**"

There was more, but it had drifted into the sort of bureaucratic jargon only postmasters and admin-loving Cogletts would care about.

"My mother is going to be *so* disappointed in me," Geartrain moaned, looking truly heartbroken.

"We haven't done anything," Dialel pointed out, entirely unbothered.

Geartrain blinked. "Oh. Right."

Hairspring gasped. "What are we going to *do*?!"

The three friends, now officially wanted criminals, began to panic—until OFT waved a calming hand.

"This… is a *good* thing."

They stared at him like he'd just suggested using the Sun as a toaster.

"Let me explain," OFT continued. "Whoever stole my green crystal also stole the clock hands. And we know there are other hands made from Excalibur. So, if we track the rest of the Excalibur pieces… we track the thief."

"But *how*?" Hairspring asked. "How do we find the other hands?"

OFT smiled and held out his palm. Nestled in it were three glowing stones.

"These."

The crystals pulsed gently, forming an arrow, twitching in unison like they were eager to be off.

"They'll guide you," OFT explained. "The closer you get to the green crystal, the brighter they'll shine—and the faster they'll move. Keep them on a chain around your neck."

He handed each of them a stone.

To Dialel, he gave a glowing red *carnelian*.

"This crystal allows you to travel forward in time—by one parri."

Next, to Hairspring, he gave a deep purple *amethyst*.

"This will let you travel back in time—also for one parri. Whatever happens in that time will only affect *you*."

Geartrain, who had discovered a suspiciously crunchy cereal made of toasted wheat weevils, had been listening with increasing excitement.

"What about me? What's mine? Is it glowing blue? Or lightning? Maybe I can fly?!" he grinned.

"To you, Geartrain, I bestow… the cat's eye quartz," OFT said, placing a small yellow pebble in his hand.

Geartrain blinked.

"That's it? It's not even a *crystal*. It's a *pebble*. With a stripe."

"This stone grants you the power of *sight*—into the past and future," OFT continued, choosing to ignore the tone.

"You mean… I can watch the football before anyone else?" Geartrain's eyes sparkled with potential.

"*NO!*" OFT barked. "Only five parri in either direction!"

Each of them clutched their stone. The crystals trembled in their hands, then—*pop!*—shifted forms.

Hairspring and Geartrain's stones morphed into tiny *sundials*, perfectly balanced and glinting.

Dialel's crystal… turned into an *egg timer*.

"Why's mine an *egg timer*?" he asked, baffled.

"I'm not sure," OFT said, frowning. "I haven't seen that happen since my days on Tempus…"

He looked thoughtful. Somewhere in his home were ancient scrolls filled with legends and histories of his people. He would need to search them—later.

Because just then, a realisation struck him.

"I know what's happening!" he gasped, just as the three were fitting the crystals around their necks.

"Whoever the thief is... they're trying to *stop the clocks*."

Dialel and Hairspring frowned.

"Stop the clocks? What does that even *mean*?" Hairspring asked before Dialel could jump in.

"If they can collect all the pieces of Excalibur," OFT explained, his face paling, "and plunge the blade into the *Queen's Wheel*... Time will *stop*. All clocks will reset. Everything will just—"

He trailed off. His expression twisted into horror.

"JUST WHAT?!" the three cried in unison.

"JUST BOOM! JUST BOOM!" shouted OFT, pacing madly. "*Everything* will go BOOM!"

This seemed like an appropriate time for an explanatory footnote... but instead, let's rewind.

Back in the 4th century, OFT had met a toy maker named Jeraint Nicholas. Every December, around the winter solstice, Jeraint would give unsold toys to children in the village of Upper North Poll. After a few mugs of very strong mulled wine, Jeraint and OFT came up with a better plan: deliver toys to *every* child in England.

Naturally, OFT said, "Why not the *world*?"

To cut a long story short, Jeraint became known as Saint Nicholas—or *Santa Claus*. Each year, he flies across the planet delivering gifts in a sleigh powered by a magical clock. The hands of that clock? Forged from Excalibur.

And if someone stole them... they could do more than stop time.

They could *end it*.

"They're heading to the North Pole," OFT whispered. "They need Nick's clock."

Geartrain was trembling with excitement.

"Wait. Let me get this straight. You… know *Santa*?!"

"Geartrain!" snapped Hairspring. "*Focus!*"

"Yeah, but it's *Santa!*" he beamed.

"No time to lose," said Dialel, gripping his egg timer like a weapon. "We need to go—*now*!"

OFT nodded. "Press the crystals between your palms."

With a brief shimmer, the three friends shrank down to Coglett size.

Dialel was already dashing for the stairs.

"I'll stay here," OFT called after them, "and guard the Master clock, the thief might want to come back for the rest of the crystals!"

Just outside, nestled by the ancient stones, a lone dandelion bloomed.

The trio leapt onto the nearest seed and were lifted skyward—rising above two security guards circling the stones, scratching their heads and muttering about missing intruders.

As the seeds caught the wind and sailed them northward, the clock was ticking—and Time, quite literally, was running out.

CHAPTER 7: A Chilly Reception

The blaring echo of the cuckoo alarm and Old Father Time's dire warning still rattled through their minds like a loose cog in a grandfather clock. Dialel, Hairspring, and Geartrain were now officially fugitives—wanted for crimes they most definitely hadn't committed, riding a seed strand through sleet and suspicion.

It was, by far, the worst flight any of them had ever taken.

Granted, Hairspring had only ever flown down the Thames, and even she was doing better than the boys. They'd been lucky early on, skimming over land as they soared north. But once they passed the northern coast of Scotland, everything got... unpleasant.

They still had over 2,200 miles to go—with nothing but the Norwegian Sea, bitter skies, and the icy silence of the Arctic shelf beneath them.

The wind was fierce, the snow relentless, and the temperature would make a brass button curl inwards.

Through it all, Geartrain repeated one mantra over and over:

"I haven't got my coat. I'm going to *catch my death*. I haven't got my coat!"

The seed strands, buffeted and battered, were barely holding together. Hairspring kept glancing at hers, worry etched across her frosted cheeks. If they didn't survive the trip, there would be no growing new ones. And no way back.

Then, just as things were reaching peak despair, a red and green light blinked through the blizzard.

It was mounted on a red and white striped pole—candy-cane themed, naturally.

"We've made it!" Dialel shouted, dismounting from his seed strand, followed quickly by Hairspring and Geartrain.

A sudden gust ripped through the clearing, whipping all three strands into the air. Hairspring lunged for hers but was too late, falling face-first into the snow.

"So… how do we get in to see *Santa*?" Geartrain asked, shivering dramatically. "And I still don't have a *coat!*"

They spotted a doorbell mounted on the pole. Below it, a sign written in elegant Elvish script.

"What do you think it says?" Dialel asked.

"Well, I haven't done Elvish since school," Hairspring muttered, squinting, "but I think it says:

PLEASE RING BELL.
NO COLD CALLERS.
PARCELS TO THE SLOT ON THE LEFT."

"No cold callers?" Geartrain grumbled. "*I'm freezing!* And… does anyone else feel like they're being tickled?"

Suddenly, their crystals began to hum.

The chains pulled taut. The gems burst from under their scarves, glowing furiously and pointing skyward.

"Someone's coming," Dialel breathed.

Two figures on seed strands were approaching from the sky.

"Whoever they are," Hairspring cried, "they've got the other crystal—quick! Into the parcel slot!"

They dove headfirst into the dark chute, sliding down a twisting tunnel that would've been great fun under *literally any other circumstances*. They landed in a soft heap of sacks, most likely labelled *Do Not Drop*.

"You're not supposed to come in that way," said a voice above them.

They looked up to see an Elf wearing a peaked hat emblazoned with:
ELF POST, ELF & SAFETY OFFICER.

"Sorry," Dialel said with a grin. "We couldn't reach the bell."

"Well, now I have to file a *Wrongly Delivered Coglett* form. In triplicate. Three copies. Because there are *three* of you!" the Elf chirped with bureaucratic joy.

"Quickly—ask him how we meet Santa!" Geartrain hissed, nudging Dialel.

"Oh, you can't meet Jerry," the Elf replied breezily. "He's *sleeping*. Big night tonight."

"We've come from OFT!" Hairspring said urgently.

"Who?"

"Old Father Time!"

"Ohhh…" the Elf trailed off. "Still no."

Then the doorbell rang.

"That's odd," the Elf said. "We don't get visitors today. Well… ever, really."

Dialel, Hairspring, and Geartrain panicked. They darted toward another door, hoping it led to Santa—or at least somewhere warm.

At the front door stood Akea and Tetia, putting on their best "respectable officials" faces.

"We're here on *urgent business*," Akea declared. "Three Cogletts have stolen the Shepards Gate clock hands. They're fugitives. Dangerous."

The Elf turned to point.

"You mean *them*?" he asked, gesturing to the squirming sacks behind him.

"They're here?" Akea gasped, eyes gleaming. He hadn't expected to bag two prizes in one sleigh ride.

"Quick! Sound the alarm!"

The Elf calmly picked up a thick clipboard. "First you'll need to fill out this form: **IN CASE OF ALARM TRIGGERING BEFORE 7PM ON CHRISTMAS EVE.**"

Akea took the form, seething. "Are all bureaucrats *like this*?!"

"You'll need a *metallic gold pen*," Tetia added helpfully.

Meanwhile, the friends had stumbled into a vast warehouse. It was filled with toys, conveyor belts, and Elves bustling like caffeinated ants. Bears in chairs, trains in paper chains, and Elves… on the floors, sewing and sorting.

"Where are we *going*?" Dialel asked.

"There!" Hairspring pointed. "That sign says: *Stables & Sleigh – This Way.*"

"Does everything rhyme here?" muttered Geartrain.

A siren sounded.

Red beacons whirled. Conveyor belts stopped mid-chug. An intercom crackled, followed by a very, very *booming* voice.

"This had better be *good!* Not another fishing trawler off Greenland!"

"Santa," Hairspring whispered. "He's awake."

Elves scrambled to block exits. Toys crashed in glorious disarray. The reindeer reared. One handler patted Rudolph's nose. ("There's a good fellow.")

The friends dove beneath a workbench.

"What's going on?!" one Elf cried.

"Maybe another Canadian whale-watching boat off Melville Island!" shouted another.

Marvin, the over-eager alarm officer, appeared looking very guilty.

"This is bad," Geartrain muttered. "Very bad. Also, I saw a present with my name on it. I *don't like Rubik's Cubes!*"

"What's the plan?" Hairspring hissed.

"I don't *have* one," Dialel admitted. "This is uncharted territory!"

"Well *I* do," Hairspring said, voice low and fierce. "That tall vending machine—if we climb up, we can see who's following us. Maybe even the other crystal."

They bolted, zig-zagging between gifts. Dialel flung his grappling hook up to the top of the machine and began to climb. The others followed.

Just as Dialel reached the top, heavy boots stomped below.

Jeriant, the Elf and Safety Officer, appeared with Akea and Tetia close behind—just out of sight. Marvin scrambled in from the other direction.

"I didn't pull the alarm, Jerry! I swear!" he squeaked.

"They're in here somewhere," Akea said. "They're after the sleigh clock!"

"We'll see about that," Jerry growled. "I need those hands to *fly tonight*!"

A search began. Elves scattered. Rudolph lit up the corners. The sleigh gleamed ominously in the background.

Then—

"What's that?" cried an Elf, pointing to the rope dangling from the vending machine.

"Oh no—the rope!" Dialel gasped.

Jerry, being the tallest person in the room (which wasn't saying much), grabbed a stool, climbed up, and peered over the top.

There they were.

He reached forward. Dialel jumped, grabbing Geartrain's crystal just in time as it fell from his snapped chain.

He landed in a pile of plushies. Jerry pulled Hairspring and Geartrain down and handed them to Akea and Tetia.

"Here you go—your criminals," he said gruffly. "Now *leave*. We've got enough chaos as it is."

"I *knew* it would be you!" Hairspring spat at Akea.

"Yes! Who else but *your* commander?" Akea sneered. "Where's Dialel?"

Trying to cover for him, Hairspring sobbed, "He's gone! A bird attacked us over the sea! He fell—we don't know where he is!"

Geartrain, taking the cue, began sobbing unconvincingly. "I miss his egg timer…"

Akea wasn't fooled—but didn't push it. He yanked the amethyst crystal from Hairspring's neck.

"I'll take this too, *thief!*"

As they turned to leave, Jerry muttered, "Merry Christmas. I'll make sure you're both on the *naughty list*."

Geartrain whimpered, "It's okay. I *hate* Rubik's Cubes."

Akea and Tetia tied Hairspring and Geartrain to the dandelion stems outside. With their prisoners in tow, they soared into the sky—disappearing into the freezing wind, leaving only frost and falling snow behind.

CHAPTER 8: Left Out In, The Cold

Dialel sat buried in a heap of soft toys, watching helplessly as his friends were dragged out of the workshop. There was nothing he could've done—if he'd moved, he'd have been caught too. But something about the Cogletts taking them didn't sit right. One of them had a gait he almost recognised.

And those uniforms… they were from Shepards Gate.

Could it really have been Tetia? And someone else?

He frowned. Surely not Akea. That oversized walking rulebook wouldn't have left his office unless the world had snapped a gear. He'd be too busy writing someone up for sneezing off-schedule.

Dialel sank back into the squishy pile, surrounded by green teddy bears that smelled faintly… of watermelon.

"Why do they smell like fruit?" he murmured, sniffing one. "Ah. Right. Because they're green."

He sighed and looked down at the crystal clutched in his palm—Geartrain's crystal. The *Cat's Eye Quartz*. The power of foresight.

Maybe, just maybe, it could show him who had taken his friends.

He stared deep into the shimmering stone. Lights began to flicker within. Then flash. Then spin. A vortex twisted inside, bouncing around as if trying to break out.

And then—it cleared.

The vision sharpened, showing Victoria train station in London.

"Wait... what's *this*?" Dialel muttered.

The view panned in toward Little Ben—the small cousin of Big Ben. The vision zoomed into one of the clock faces.

There was Akea.

He was shouting, "*Hurry! It's nearly midnight—we must stop them!*"

The image blinked out.

"What the broken wrist strap was that?!" Dialel said aloud, his voice bouncing off the toys.

Clutching Geartrain's crystal to his chest, he felt a strange warmth grow in his hand. His own crystal, still hanging from his neck, began to glow in response.

"Oh great. What now?"

The crystal in his hand grew hotter. He dropped it, but not before it scorched a neat little hole in his shirt. The two stones touched—red and yellow—and the heat grew unbearable. It was as though time itself had weight, and it was pinning him to the belly of a watermelon-scented bear.

Then—*FLASH!* A white light burst from the pile of toys.

Where there were two crystals, now there was one—fused into a brilliant orange *egg timer.*

An Elf—small, spritely, and suspicious—had noticed the glowing from the toy pile and came running.

She had good reason. The last time someone made glowing plushies, they'd tried to make *Scotch Bonnet Chilli Bears.* They had spontaneously combusted. It was a *whole* thing.

She yanked away the top layer of bears and gasped.

"Who are you?! What are you doing in these bears?! Are you another troublemaker?! What happened to your shirt?! The bears didn't *burn* you, did they?!"

"Whoa, whoa, whoa!" Dialel held up his hands. "I'm a Coglett. My name is Dialel. I need to see Santa!"

The Elf squinted at him.

"Santa?" she asked, then clicked. "Oh, you mean Jerry. Everyone else calls him Santa. Right. He's *sleeping*—it's Christmas Eve, you know."

"Yes, I know! That's *why* I'm here!" Dialel said desperately.

"You could've sent a letter like *everyone else.* We get thousands. 'Can I have this?' 'Can I have that?' Honestly…"

Dialel had had enough.

"This is important. *Take me to him. Now. PLEASE!*"

"No need to shout," she huffed. "Follow me. You're very short, aren't you?"

As she turned, Dialel climbed out of the toys and—*whoosh!*—grew to full height.

"Impressive," the Elf said. "Do all of you grow like that?"

Dialel shrugged and said nothing.

They wandered down a corridor that looked like a wrapping-paper tornado had passed through. Ribbon, tape, and glitter balls rolled underfoot. They stopped at a door with a gleaming brass sign that read:

THE LIST (in exquisite calligraphy, naturally).

"He'll be in there. Been in once already today," the Elf said, walking away.

"Aren't you going to introduce me?" Dialel called after her.

"No need. He'll know your name. Bit odd like that," she replied over her shoulder.

Dialel knocked.

"Come in!" bellowed a voice. "And this had better *not* be another problem!"

He stepped inside.

"Hello, I'm Dial—"

"Dialel," interrupted Jerry. "Porth Mawgan, right? No—wait, you're stationed at Shepards Gate now, aren't you?"

Dialel blinked. "Y-yes, that's right."

Bit creepy.

"Call me Jerry. Everyone else does. Now, you'd better not be with those *other two*. They're on my Naughty List."

"Actually, yes... I *am*," Dialel confessed.

"WHAT?! You're with *Tetia* and—oh what's his name—hang on." Jerry grabbed a heavy book labelled *COGLETT DIRECTORY – SOUTH ENGLAND*.

"No! Not *them*—I was with the two they *took*! Geartrain and Hairspring."

"Oh, that's different then," Jerry relaxed. "I like that Geartrain—funny chap. He's getting a Rubik's Cube for Christmas!"

Dialel winced. "He *hates* those."

Jerry waved him off. "Look, it's lovely to have visitors, but it's Christmas Eve. We're flat out. Do you *know* what it's like to do an entire year's work in one night?"

Dialel climbed onto a stack of books beside the desk.

"This is really important. End-of-the-world important. Old Father Time sent us!"

And so Dialel explained everything that had happened so far. (If *you*, dear reader, don't recall everything, please return to Chapter One. We'll wait.)

Jerry listened, mouth slightly agape.

"That's… serious," he muttered. "Right. Come on. We're starting the work early."

"Work? What work?" asked Dialel as they jogged through the corridors.

"You told me you've got no way to get home," Jerry said. "So, I'll give you the ride."

They reached the stables.

In front of them stood the most spectacular sleigh Dialel had ever seen—carved wood, golden swirls, twinkling lanterns. Elves swarmed around it wearing jackets that said **PIT CREW**.

On the dashboard sat a magnificent clock.

Its case was ajar, and inside—somehow both dramatically and casually—stood a very old Coglett.

"How do, young fella?" he said, tipping an imaginary hat.

"I'm good, thanks. Yourself?" Dialel replied automatically.

"This is Rolax," Jerry said. "He built this clock. Back when OFT hid the Excalibur."

Dialel's jaw dropped. *Rolax*. One of the *first* Truids to land on Earth.

Jerry barked orders. Nine reindeer appeared, almost like magic.

"This, my boy," said Jerry, waving grandly, "is how we're getting you home. We'll just have to make a few million stops on the way."

Rolax hopped down from the sleigh.

The barn doors creaked open.

Jerry and Dialel climbed aboard.

Jeriant the Elf and Safety officer, appeared and handed Dialel a coat. "You'll need this."

As Dialel shrugged it on, Rolax spotted something around his neck.

"*THE CRYSTAL!*" he shouted. "Where did you get it?!"

Dialel opened his mouth to explain—

Crack!

Jerry snapped the reins.

(He would never hit the reindeer. That's rude. The sound was for dramatic flair.)

The sleigh surged forward.

Rolax watched it go, still staring at the orange crystal.

He hadn't seen one since Tempus.

And the last person to wear one… was Akea's father.

CHAPTER 9: You've Done the Crime, Now You Do the Time

Geartrain and Hairspring had been returned to London, dragged (without so much as a courtesy whistle-stop) directly to the Tower of London by Akea and Tetia.

Geartrain was in an abysmal state—utterly inconsolable. Not because they were prisoners. Not because they were accused of crimes they hadn't committed. But because he was certain—absolutely certain—that Santa was going to deliver him a Rubik's Cube.

Hairspring, on the other hand, had no time for puzzles or panic. She paced in the cell next door, scanning every nook for a possible way out or some sort of ancient Coglett mail chute. It was well into Christmas Eve, and from the small barred window all she could see were humans darting about in a festive frenzy—men clutching poorly chosen gifts, children being dragged through crowds like reluctant sleds, and merry revellers who seemed to think that wearing antlers in public was normal behaviour.

Hairspring wasn't in the mood for celebrating. She didn't know where Dialel was or whether he was safe. And as for Geartrain—if he mentioned that Rubik's Cube *one more time*, she was going to... well, something dramatic and possibly involving a hot custard pie.

Outside the cells, in a grimy corridor that smelled faintly of mildew and history, she could just make out the voices of Akea and Tetia.

"It's fine," Akea was explaining in his usual smug, spreadsheet-loving tone. "We'll have enough of the steel we need once we get the hands from Little Ben."

Who is Little Ben? Hairspring wondered. She didn't know if it was a person, a clock, or a badly named garden gnome.

"Yeah, yeah, I get that bit," Tetia replied. "But I still don't understand the rest. How does sticking a tatty old sword into a bunch of old stones save an island in the middle of the Pacific?"

Hairspring leaned in, ear to the door. A chair scraped against the floor.

"Right," Akea said, voice sharpening. "Listen carefully, as I shall say this only once more."

Hairspring rolled her eyes. He said that every time. Then repeated himself anyway.

"According to my father's notebook, if we can gather enough of the sword, we can reforge Excalibur. Then we take it to Stonehenge, and I plunge it—dramatically, I might add—into the centre of the monoliths. As you know, Stonehenge is actually a clock—"

Suddenly, Geartrain sneezed from his cell. Loudly.

"Excuse me! Have you got any tissues? I appear to have made a bit of a mess!" he shouted.

Hairspring groaned. *Oh, for the love of cogs.*

Akea stomped over, slid the shutter on the cell door open, and glared at Geartrain.

"This is *not* a hotel," he barked. "You're not here on your holidays!"

Geartrain gave a weak laugh. "Wouldn't book this place anyway. Sheets haven't been changed in years, and the food—Michelin stars? More like Michelin rubber."

Akea frowned. "You haven't *had* any food."

Geartrain blinked. "Then what was that grey mush on the plate in the corner when I got here?"

Akea cackled with villainous satisfaction, then repeated his order to stay quiet and stormed off. Tetia, still at the table, was snorting with laughter.

"What do you think he ate?" he asked.

"No idea," Akea replied. "Now, where was I...? Oh yes. Sticking the sword into the stone."

He cleared his throat. "As you know, there's one particular stone in the centre of the circle. It's the core of the Master Clock. When I plunge the blade into it, time will stop."

"Stop?" Tetia blinked.

"Exactly!" Akea's eyes gleamed. "Time will freeze. We'll have as long as we need to reset the clocks and restart everything. And do you know when we'll start it from?" He paused, then whispered dramatically, *"Zero."*

Then he burst into maniacal laughter.

"I'll return to the exact moment the volcano swallowed Vizibaltia, stop it from erupting, and *save my island*! All of it. Back the way it was!"

They left the room in high spirits, presumably off to gloat in fresher air. Hairspring, having heard every word, stood frozen by the door.

"Great," she muttered. "He's not just a power-hungry bureaucrat—he's a full-blown *clock-crazy time tyrant*."

But now what? She didn't know how to escape. She didn't know where Dialel was. And she certainly didn't know how to warn OFT.

Then she heard it: a scraping sound. Followed by someone being violently (and suspiciously) sick.

The scraping grew louder—then a small brick in the wall popped loose.

It had come from Geartrain's side.

"Hello? You okay?" Geartrain's voice floated through, casual as anything.

"What are you *doing*?" Hairspring hissed.

"I just wanted to make sure you were alright."

"I thought you were *being sick*!"

"Oh, that? No, just pretending. Didn't want them to hear me breaking the wall. I trained as a clock tower structural engineer, you know. These cells are ancient. Loose bricks, crumbly mortar—it's practically a renovation opportunity."

Hairspring stared at the brick in disbelief.

"So have you found a way out? Can we get a message to OFT?" she asked, breath catching with hope.

"Oh... no. Still a prison," Geartrain admitted. "But I thought maybe, since we only have each other, we could... I don't know. Talk?"

She blinked at the hole.

"You... broke through a *wall*... just so we could talk?"

"Well, yeah. I figured you were as worried about Dialel as I am. And I thought—if we could at least see each other, it might help. You know, comfort and camaraderie and all that."

He reached through and gently held her hand.

Then, in true Geartrain fashion, he added, "That Akea's a few cogs short of a full clock, don't you think?"

Hairspring laughed—properly, for the first time in what felt like days.

They practised pushing the brick in and out, turning it into a little game, timing each other. They even managed to make it fun. For a moment, it felt like old times.

Then footsteps echoed down the corridor.

"Quick—brick!" Geartrain whispered.

They shoved it back into place just as the floor shutters clanked open. A tray of food slid in.

"Lights out in fifteen parri," called a voice they didn't recognise.

Meanwhile, Akea and Tetia stood atop the Tower's ramparts, overlooking the Thames, wrapped in shadow and ambition.

"Where is Dialel?" Akea wondered aloud.

They hadn't seen him since the North Pole. The other two wouldn't talk. Not yet, at least.

But no matter. They had a schedule to keep, a sword to complete, and a plan to execute. The hands from Little Ben were next. And then—Stonehenge.

Tick. Tock. Time was running out.

CHAPTER 10: Your Delivery Will Be at...

Santa (also known to a select few as *Jerry*) had started work about an hour earlier than usual. Not because of weather, or sleigh delays, or an elf strike (although Marvin had recently attempted to unionise the sleigh bells), but because he needed to get Dialel back to London.

Now, it's extremely hard to explain exactly how Jerry's magic works. But here's a rough idea—somewhere between 'scientifically implausible' and 'festively fantastic'.

You see, Rolax—the clockmaker, time-tinkerer, and occasional soup enthusiast—had created the first and only functioning time-machine. Not one of those clunky things you see in films, with flux capacitors or spinning dials and a dashboard that looks like it came from a microwave. No, no, *this* machine had the uncanny ability to freeze time in micro-fractions of a Parri.

And as we know (or at least, *should* know), sixty Parri is the equivalent of one human minute. Rolax's machine could stop time every tenth of a Parri and then start it again two-tenths later. The effect on reality was, quite frankly, unfathomable. Which is exactly why some people don't believe in Santa.

Because, really, why would you believe that a man weighing eighteen stone—give or take a few mince pies—could fly around the world, visit 195 countries in a single night, powered only by reindeer and jolly determination?

But *we* believe, don't we?

—

Dialel and Jerry were just finishing up the very last delivery on one of the final tiny islands—a snowy speck off the edge of the Aleutian chain. A small girl named Anastasiia would soon wake to find her gift under the tree. She wouldn't know, of course, that she was the *last* delivery of the night.

Or so it seemed.

Jerry's sack still held *three* more parcels.

Dialel frowned, watching the landscape blur beneath them. "Why didn't you drop me off when we flew over London earlier?"

"Ahhh, we didn't have time," Jerry said, adjusting his mittens. "Well, we *had* time, but not the *kind* of time we needed. You see, although this sleigh is something special, and yes, it bends time like a spoon in a wizard's pudding, we don't have *full* control. That, my new friend, belongs to Old Father Time—and the Master Clock at Stonehenge."

Dialel's mind snapped to OFT and the tale of the war on Tempus. The artefacts. The Druigs. The ticking threat.

"Then there's no time to waste!" he shouted. "We have to get to London! Hairspring and Geartrain—they could be in danger! Tetia's involved, I *know* it!"

Jerry's eyes twinkled. "That's easy, my boy. Ho-ho-ho."

Dialel raised an eyebrow. "That doesn't actually answer my question."

"Ah, but the presents will," Jerry replied with a grin. "No gift is ever truly lost. They'll guide us. Grab those three from the sack."

Dialel reached into the bag and pulled out three wrapped gifts—one each for Hairspring, Geartrain, and… himself.

"You can open yours," Jerry said, eyes twinkling even more now. "Go on."

Dialel hesitated. He glanced at the sleigh's dashboard clock. Did they really have time for this?

"*Go on!*" Jerry urged.

Dialel tore open the wrapping. Inside was a beautiful blue velvet box. He popped open the ornate clasp, and inside sat a silver pocket watch, glinting like moonlight on ice.

On the back, engraved in swirling script, it read:

Hands cut through time.
A pendulum swings, making bells ring.
Tic-toc, the clock must not stop.

Dialel opened it. The face was unlike any he'd ever seen—split like a four-leaf clover, with the clock dial at its centre.

At once, the crystals around his neck began to writhe beneath his shirt, glowing brighter, hotter. They surged against the fabric, desperate to escape. Dialel quickly pulled the chain over his head—he wasn't about to get scorched again.

The sleigh filled with light.

There was a deafening crack, like a thunderclap inside a snow globe.

The red crystal leapt into the top slot of the watch. Geartrain's yellow cat's eye slid into place beside the three. The clock face shimmered—changing from white to a deep, pulsing orange.

The watch flipped closed and sat, humming gently, in Dialel's palm.

Jerry's jaw dropped. "Well, butter my boots… I have *no* idea where that came from! You were meant to be getting a climbing rope!"

Dialel blinked at the glowing pocket watch. "Honestly, the way things are going, I think I'd have preferred the rope."

Still staring at the thing, he added, "But… this must be OFT's doing."

Jerry shook his head in wonder. "Well then. No time like the present."

"Pun intended?" Dialel smirked.

"Always."

Jerry pointed to a drawer labelled:
GIFT FINDER ONLY. NOT TO BE USED AS A SAT-NAV.

"Pop Hairspring's present in there."

Dialel obeyed. The moment the drawer closed, a small screen lit up on the dashboard. A satellite view of Earth zoomed in—spinning and spinning—until it honed in on England... then London... then a familiar, formidable structure on the Thames:

The Tower of London.

"There! They're inside," Jerry cried. He cracked the whip (again, theatrically, not violently), and the reindeer surged forward with an almighty jingle.

—

Meanwhile, in a quiet house back on the Aleutian Islands, Anastasiia crept downstairs. Her slippers made barely a sound on the floor.

She spotted it immediately—a gift wrapped in gleaming red and gold paper.

She gasped.

She opened it.

And found the very present she had asked Santa for.

Because she believed.

And somewhere, in the skies above the world, a sleigh was streaking towards the Tower of London.

Because sometimes, belief is all the magic you need.

CHAPTER 11: Break Time

The sun had just begun to rise over London, its light glinting off the Shard and making the towering skyscraper appear like an enormous wax candle, freshly lit and flickering across the city. Unseen by the sleepy-eyed commuters and tourists sipping lukewarm coffee, Jerry and Dialel soared silently past it in the sleigh, heading towards Tower Bridge.

Bringing the sleigh to a halt atop the bridge (a rather showy parking spot, but Jerry liked flair), they peered down at the shadowy expanse of the Tower of London.

"Where could they be in there?" Dialel asked, shielding his eyes from the sun.

"If I had to guess," Jerry replied, pointing across the courtyard with a jolly seriousness, "the North Tower—overlooking the moat. That's where they usually stick people when they've been *falsely accused of crimes against time and Christmas.*"

Dialel frowned. He had no plan. No backup. Just an overdeveloped sense of duty, an orange time-altering pocket watch, and a very questionable track record with punctuality.

"I've got to go," Jerry said, patting the sleigh with affection. "The reindeers have flown farther tonight than ever before. They're knackered." With a final crack of the whip and a festive "Ho-ho-hope you survive!" Jerry and the sleigh vanished into the dawn.

Dialel was left blinking at empty sky and wondering how he was going to climb the massive walls surrounding the tower holding his imprisoned friends.

Luckily, down by the tower, a rogue patch of weeds had sprouted up between some forgotten cobblestones. And nestled among them? Dandelions.

Dialel grinned.

He plucked a stem, said a little thank you to whichever botany spirit was watching over him, and hurled himself off the bridge.

—

The flight was... less than smooth. The dandelion seed was wild and untrained—like trying to fly a bucking goat on a windy day. Dialel bounced and spun through the air like a biscuit in a tumble dryer. He fought to steer it towards the far tower Jerry had pointed out, grabbing his rope and lobbing the grappling hook over a spire. He let go of the seed and swung towards the tower roof.

The landing was not elegant.

He slid off the curved slates and only narrowly avoided plummeting into the moat, thanks to his belt and a lucky knot on the rope.

As he dangled awkwardly from the side of the tower, grunting and trying to regain composure, he suddenly felt the rope jerk upwards.

He looked up.

A Tower raven was hauling him to safety with determined flaps, a Coglett guard straddling its back like a miniature knight. The guard wore a glorious green uniform—part Beefeater, part bird-whisperer.

Dialel, panting, rolled onto the ledge. "Thank you! I thought I was about to become moat soup."

"I am a Guardian of the Crown Jewels," the Coglett announced grandly. "Specifically, the King's Pocket Watch. But I'm afraid I'm going to have to arrest you now."

"Arrest me?" Dialel blinked. "For what?"

"You didn't enter the Tower via the Clockface Crown Access Point. Nor did you register your presence or declare your temporal intentions. So... yes. Arrested." He sniffed, clearly the type to keep an alphabetised list of protocols.

"And you may be connected to those two that tried to stop Santa and delay Christmas."

Dialel blinked. *Oh.* So the guard was talking about Geartrain and Hairspring.

"Well then," Dialel said, channelling his best melodrama. "It's a fair cop. I confess. Better lock me up before I commit a heinous act of present mis-delivery. "

The guard looked confused but pleased. "Well. That's refreshingly cooperative."

He whispered into the raven's ear. The bird jerked upright, tightened its grip on the rope in its beak, and flapped mightily. Down they went—plunging through what appeared to be an old rain outlet in the wall. Inside, the raven landed and pinned Dialel gently to the ground with one claw, like a cat holding down a particularly wriggly mouse.

The guard hopped down, tied Dialel's hands with the rope, and marched him through a series of dark tunnels. Eventually, he unlocked a door and shoved Dialel inside.

"I'll be back shortly to take you to the Commander. Don't touch anything."

He slammed the door.

On a rickety bed sat a short, slightly tubby Coglett with an enormous grin and unruly hair that practically screamed *'used to better sheets.'*

"GEARTRAIN!" Dialel gasped.

"DIALEL!" Geartrain squealed, leaping up and tackling him with a hug that could dislocate ribs.

"How did you get here?" Geartrain said. "Last I saw, you were still in the North Pole and Ak—"

A scraping noise interrupted him. A loose brick slid aside.

"What's going on?!" came Hairspring's voice, tinny and distorted through the wall.

"It's Dialel!" Geartrain called.

"BUT HOW?!" came the disembodied hand and accompanying confusion.

"I was just about to tell you," Dialel said, straightening up.

He recounted everything—his ride with Jerry, the sleigh, Rolax, the sleigh-clock, the orange watch. Everything. Including not knowing who had captured them.

Hairspring and Geartrain shared what they'd overheard about Akea and Tetia's plan: steal the hands from Little Ben, head to Stonehenge, and somehow *stop time.*

Dialel looked horrified. "We have to stop them. But first—we need to get out."

"I know how!" came the faceless hand, now pointing triumphantly.

—

THE PLAN

1. Dialel and Geartrain would ambush the guard.
2. Grab the keys.
3. Free Hairspring.
4. Escape through the Tower, reach Tower Hill tube station.
5. Ride the Circle Line to Victoria.

"Sounds easy," Geartrain said. "I love trains. I hope Jerry got me a train set for Christmas."

"I'm sure whatever it is... you'll love it," Dialel lied.

They braced themselves.

The key scraped in the lock.

Geartrain, holding a pillowcase like a net, stood behind the door. Dialel stood front and centre, all innocence and false compliance.

The door creaked open.

The guard stepped in.

THWOMP—the pillowcase went over the guard's head.

THUMP—Dialel dropped down and tripped him.

WHUMP—Geartrain pushed, Dialel pounced, the guard flailed.

"Run!" Geartrain shouted, snatching the keys.

They slammed the door, locked it, and raced to Hairspring's cell. The keys jingled. The lock clicked. The door opened.

The reunion hug was, naturally, *epic.*

"This way!" Dialel led them through the same passage the guard had brought him down.

But then—

THE RAVEN.

It stood in the middle of the corridor like a feathery sentinel of doom.

"WHAT NOW?!" Dialel gasped.

"THIS!" said Geartrain, leaping onto the raven's back.

"GET ON!"

They scrambled aboard.

The raven flapped, took off, and soared through the Tower's outer wall and into the open air, over tourists and pigeons, over camera phones and confused gasps, and landed on the entrance roof of the Tube station.

"Off you get," Geartrain said, sliding down.

"How... how did you *do* that?" Dialel asked, wide-eyed.

"Oh, I read a book," Geartrain shrugged. "If the ravens ever leave the Tower, the kingdom falls. And turns out, they're also fantastic public transport."

Hairspring whispered to Dialel, "I'm learning all kinds of weird things about Geartrain."

Dialel nodded. "He's like a walking, sniffling, moaning mystery novel."

They dashed into the Tube station and raced for the platforms below.

Stonehenge—and Little Ben—were calling.

Chapter 12: The Race is On

Back in the Tower, the sound of heavy boots on cold stone echoed ominously as Akea and Tetia burst into the now-empty cells. A frantic banging was coming from one of them—Geartrain's, or so they thought—only to find a furious Tower guard shouting through the bars.

"They've escaped! All three of them!"

Akea froze mid-step. Tetia skidded to a halt beside him.

"Three? Did you say three?" Akea growled, his voice suddenly tight with disbelief.

The guard blinked, confused. "Uh... yes? Two cells. Three gone. That's math, right?"

The blood drained from Akea's face. No one had told them Dialel was here. The guard had never registered a third prisoner.

"They know," Akea whispered, almost to himself. "They know everything."

Tetia's voice cracked as panic crept in. "What are we going to do now?"

"What are we—what are *we* going to do?" Akea snapped, spinning to face him. "You imbecile! We do what we were always going to do—we get to Little Ben. *Before* those malfunctioning minute hands get there first!"

"But surely, they won't get far, right? They can't be that smart," Tetia offered weakly.

The guard scoffed. "You mean the three who escaped a fortified tower undetected? Yeah... real dim bulbs, those ones."

Akea's eye twitched. With a furious scream, he grabbed a chipped mug off the table and hurled it at the wall—where it shattered into a dozen sharp regrets.

"IDIOT!" he roared. "There were only *two* cells! Who *is* the third?! How did they even get in?!"

"I've had it with this chaos," the guard muttered. "Ever since you two turned up, it's been nothing but madness. I didn't sign up for this—I'm meant to polish pocket watches, not chase magical fugitives."

With fire in his eyes and a storm brewing in his brain, Akea spun on his heel and stormed from the cellblock, dragging Tetia by the sleeve. His carefully orchestrated plan—the one he'd spent countless Parri perfecting—was unravelling. Everything was spinning wildly *anti-clockwise*.

They had to reach Little Ben first. No more delays. No more mishaps.

Akea tapped his temple repeatedly. "Think... think... THINK!"

Then he stopped. He turned to Tetia and screamed—more out of panic than rage, "How are we going to get there in time?!"

Tetia blinked. "Umm... we could call a Zoosh?"

A beat of silence. Akea's eye twitched again.

"A *what*?"

"A Zoosh. It's like a human taxi, but for us. Faster. Quieter. Much more explodey if you sneeze mid-ride."

Akea seized Tetia by the lapels. "I KNOW WHAT A TAXI IS! HOW DO YOU GET ONE?!"

"Easy," Tetia said, now slightly enjoying his turn to lead. He tapped on his new Tangerine watch. A few glowing tiles lit up. With a swipe and a tap, a message popped onto the screen.

"Driver's name is Papel. Arrival in two Parri. Rooftop pick-up."

"Rooftop? What sort of nonsense—never mind. MOVE!"

They dashed up the winding staircases, bursting through the rooftop door just in time to see the sky ripple and shimmer as a sleek, arrow-shaped vehicle materialised from nothing.

A window zipped down.

"Yo, I'm Papel. Tetia? You're late. Get in, we ain't got all millennium."

Akea blinked, speechless. The door *hissed* open with a dramatic whisper.

They jumped in.

Now, a Zoosh is nothing like a taxi humans would ever comprehend. It doesn't drive. It doesn't fly. It *zooms* through *Parri*—folding time like a neatly ironed handkerchief.

"Where to?" Papel asked, flipping switches with the nonchalance of someone who could—and frequently did—accidentally warp a continent.

"Little Ben. Victoria Station." Akea barked.

"Hold tight then."

There was a flash. A boom. Possibly a second reality hiccupping in protest.

Akea squinted out the window. "Was that… the Statue of Liberty?"

"No," Tetia frowned, "Taj Mahal?"

Thud. The Zoosh stopped. They both flew forward into the timeproof safety glass.

"I told you to hold on."

They stepped out—dazed, slightly flatter—and stood atop the gantry hanging over Victoria Station. Below them, across the pedestrian square, stood the clock: small, black, noble. *Little Ben.*

But they weren't alone.

Down below, unseen but scrambling with purpose, Dialel, Hairspring, and Geartrain were darting through the shadows of Tower Hill Station. Breathless and bruised, they pelted down the escalators like three particularly determined buttons rolling off a too-tight waistcoat.

They hit the platform—*WHAM*—just as the train roared in. Wind sent them tumbling like breadcrumbs in a hurricane.

"Grab the rope!" Dialel shouted as Geartrain slid toward the edge.

Hairspring latched on. Dialel anchored himself to the platform tile. Geartrain squealed, disappearing over the lip—

SNAP! The rope held.

Geartrain dangled like a poorly timed bauble until they hauled him up in one adrenaline-fuelled heave.

As the train hissed and its doors slid open, they tumbled inside and collapsed behind a suitcase.

"Nine stops," Hairspring gasped, counting. "We've got nine stops."

"I hope they don't know we're free," Geartrain mumbled.

They were wrong.

Akea and Tetia crouched above Little Ben, scanning the plaza.

And just beneath them, behind a water hydrant sign, three familiar Coglett heads peeked out of the shadows.

Across the plaza, the clock loomed, quietly ticking the seconds away.

Five Cogletts.

One artefact.

Two missions.

And time?

Time was running out.

Chapter 13: Hickory Dickory Dock They All Run Up the Clock

Dialel crouched behind the water hydrant sign, heart pounding louder than any chime he'd ever cleaned. Above him, red buses rumbled, taxis tooted, and humans shuffled past with gift bags, coffee cups, and an utter lack of awareness that a clock-based war was teetering on the brink of chaos just beneath their very feet.

"I can see all the hands on the clock… except the one on the far side," he whispered, squinting at Little Ben through the forest of ankles and advertising boards.

Hairspring frowned in concentration. "If only we had the crystals that Old Father Time gave us! We could've used them somehow!"

Dialel's eyes lit up. "That's it! Hairspring, you genius!"

"I've lost mine," Geartrain confessed with a sorrowful wobble of the lip. "Haven't seen it since we tried to hide in Jerry's workshop."

Dialel reached into his pocket and triumphantly pulled out the yellow glimmer of Geartrain's cat's eye crystal. "Wrong again, my forgetful friend—I grabbed it before they dragged you away!"

Hairspring clapped her hands. "Perfect! Yours moves us forward in time, Dialel, and Geartrain's lets us go back—but only one Parri. So if we mess up… we can try again!"

Meanwhile, above the chaos and curry-scented air, Akea and Tetia crouched on a rooftop, their eyes scanning Little Ben like hawks tracking prey. Akea's lip curled into a sinister grin.

"There," he said, pointing to the gutter. "Wild seed strands. Not ideal—but they'll fly."

They scrambled across the roof, snatched up the scraggly dandelions, and launched themselves into the air just as a rogue café vent blasted a gust of chip-fat heat, sending them tumbling upwards in a whirl of wings, fur, and shrieked profanity.

Down below, Dialel and crew played a very real game of life-sized Frogger, leaping between newspaper pages, suitcases, and rogue pigeons. Every movement was a gamble—one wrong step and they'd be bird food, chewing gum, or worse... late.

As they reached the base of Little Ben, a silver glint caught Hairspring's eye. "There!" she hissed. A door—small, dusty, invisible to human eyes—waited like a secret invitation.

Dialel yanked the handle. "It's locked!"

Geartrain huffed and elbowed past. "Let me try!" He gave the door a determined shove... and promptly fell through it as it creaked open under his weight. "It says *push* right there," he muttered, brushing himself off. "Honestly, it's like working with toddlers."

High above, inside the clock, Akea and Tetia hit the landing zone hard. Their wild descent sent paperwork, spanners, and at least one half-eaten pasty flying.

"I need to see the Oscillator!" Akea barked before the landing crew could stop spinning. "Emergency!"

Downstairs, the trio began the steep spiral climb. Geartrain groaned at the first step. "This is absurd. My knees weren't built for this."

"Neither was your mouth," Hairspring shot back. "Keep climbing!"

Above, the Oscillator's scowl could have boiled a kettle and made a very un-drinkable cup of tea . "You interrupted my siesta. This had better be good."

Akea launched into his rehearsed lie, tongue gliding like a greasy gear: "Criminal Cogletts. Sheppard's Gate. After your clock hands."

The Oscillator turned pale. "They must be stopped. At all costs."

Meanwhile, three friends had just hit the halfway mark on the staircase when Hairspring gasped, "Why didn't we use the crystals?!"

Too late. The trap was already sprung.

Back inside, Akea, ever the manipulator, turned toward the guards. "Did you hear that?"

The guards glanced around. "Hear what?"

"There it is again!" Akea pointed into a dark corner and gave Tetia the most theatrical wink imaginable.

Off dashed the guards. Akea yanked open the clock face door, pulled out the crystal he'd stolen from Hairspring and held it aloft. There was a green shimmer, a sound like a music box uncoiling too quickly, and the clock hands vanished.

Two thin black shards—once the very limbs of time—lay nestled on the ledge. Akea snatched them up, heart hammering with victory. "We've got them! Let's go!"

Moments later, the trapdoor creaked open and Dialel's head popped up like a startled jack-in-the-box. The trio burst into the clock face room—just in time to find it empty.

"They've taken the hands," Hairspring whispered.

From below, footsteps thundered upward.

"Time to go!" Dialel shouted.

"Too late!" Geartrain shouted back. "Unless—"

He pulled the cat's eye crystal from his collar, slammed it into the air, and the room twisted, shimmered, and reversed—taking them back a Parri, just before they opened the door.

"Still too late," Hairspring gasped. "But we know where they're going."

Dialel nodded grimly. "Stonehenge."

"There was a bus outside," Hairspring said suddenly. "STONEHENGE AND AMESBURY. It was on the sign!"

She turned and leapt down the staircase, dragging the boys behind her.

Up above, the room lay quiet… empty… except for the dust motes floating in the sunbeam through the window, and the ticking absence of Little Ben's missing hands.

The race wasn't just on anymore. The final leg had begun.

Chapter 14: It's the Final Countdown

The bus wheezed and gasped its last breath of diesel-scented determination as it rolled to a stop outside the Stonehenge visitor centre, like a tired dragon who had seen better millennia.

As the doors creaked open and tourists spilled out like slightly damp laundry, Dialel peered from beneath the luggage compartment, pointing dramatically (as heroes tend to do) towards the ancient monoliths that stood resolute across the road.

"There! That's it! We're here!" he exclaimed.

"Finally," Hairspring muttered, brushing stray bus fluff from her jacket. "If Geartrain had asked *'Are we there yet?'* one more time, I swear on all the ticking towers I'd have thrown him under the rear wheels."

"Well," Geartrain sniffed, "that would've been tricky, seeing as there weren't any windows. Or indeed seatbelts. Or even... seats."

They hurried toward the road, dodging crisp packets, chewing gum, and the general debris of modern tourism. A helpful, if slightly smug, clock informed them it was 3 p.m.—just ninety minutes until sunset, and destiny. (Give or take a cup of tea.)

They dashed across the tarmac like fugitives from a cuckoo clock gone rogue. Just as they reached the middle of the road, an enormous articulated lorry rounded the corner, roaring like a steel banshee on wheels.

Geartrain froze.

"You know how rabbits freeze in headlights?" said Dialel, already sprinting. "Well, he's more like a squirrel in a fuse box!"

The truck thundered past, missing Geartrain by mere inches, though the **draft** did not. It picked him up like a napkin in a wind tunnel and flung him—pirouetting, flailing and yelping—over Dialel and Hairspring's heads. He landed in a clump of grass, dizzy and stunned, looking up at the sky as if it might explain itself.

"I *never* want to do that again," he wheezed.

"Impressive form," Dialel noted. "A double somersault with a yelp. Very stylish."

Geartrain glared.

As he picked himself up, something glittered in the grass—a crystal, his crystal, flung loose in the aerial drama. He reached for it, accidentally activated it, and—*fwip!*—was thrown through the air again.

"I *said* never again!" he bellowed, tumbling like magical laundry.

They made it, bruised and breathless, to the hidden entrance beneath the ancient stones. Dialel thumped on the marker just as OFT had before, and with a rumble and a hiss of ancient enchantment, the staircase opened into the Earth.

"OFT!" Dialel shouted as they descended. "We've got trouble! Big, horrible, smug trouble!"

Old Father Time stood at the bottom, unphased and drinking tea that looked older than most of the planet's mountains.

"Oh, it's you," he said, raising a brow. "About time."

They filled him in—Akea, Tetia, the hands, the crystals, the plan to shatter reality like an over-wound watch spring.

"They have the blade," Dialel concluded.

"But not the hilt," OFT said smugly, tapping his staff.

"The hilt?" asked Hairspring.

"Handle," OFT said, raising the staff aloft like the world's most elegant walking stick. "This."

"But what if they *get* the staff?" she asked, worried.

"They won't," OFT said firmly. "We'll stop them."

"Could've done that earlier," muttered Geartrain, brushing grass from his ears. "I mean, I've been flung, kidnapped, bus-wedged and imprisoned. And I *still* don't know what I'm getting for Christmas."

OFT simply smiled. "Because, my time-tossed friend, everything had to happen exactly as it did. Now, come. The sun's nearly down. And so is my patience."

They emerged between the ancient stones just as the last light began to stretch across the sky—and there, silhouetted in the glow, stood two very unwelcome silhouettes.

Akea and Tetia.

"We've been expecting you," Akea sneered, lifting a crystal in one hand and, with a flick, zapping OFT out of existence. *Poof.* Gone. Like a clock that suddenly realised it was digital.

"Well," muttered Geartrain to Dialel, "he said he could stop them…"

Another flick of the wrist, and Geartrain vanished too, shouting something about unfair crystal-based abductions.

Dialel and Hairspring scattered, diving behind the stones as the sky above them darkened—not from nightfall, but from the magical storm Akea was conjuring. It swirled above Stonehenge like a very punctual apocalypse.

With theatrical flair, Akea assembled the pieces. The hands from Little Ben formed a blade. The Shepton Gate hands became a crossguard. OFT's staff slotted in as the hilt.

"All we need now," he grinned maniacally, "is the pommel!"

"Oh, we've got that," Tetia confirmed, producing the crystal.

Then Akea raised his hand and began to chant.

*"Point to the twelve, point to the six.
Join them together, so the time sticks.
Point to the three, point to the nine.
Return to the stone, to reset the time!"*

The sky exploded with green lightning, swirling clouds now forming a vortex directly above the stones. Time itself was wobbling. Ticking. Teetering on the brink.

Dialel turned to Hairspring. "We need a plan."

"I've got one," she said. "We improvise!"

As Akea cackled, surrounded by floating clock hands and dramatic weather, Dialel hurled his grappling rope up the stone with a hero's hope. By some miracle, it caught.

He swung up, bouncing off stone like a miniature action hero, just as Hairspring tackled Tetia with the grace and force of a particularly determined squirrel.

Akea was too far gone to notice. Green lightning struck the assembled sword.

FLASH.

Time screamed.

Dialel reached the summit, spinning his rope like a lasso. He threw. It struck the hilt.

And exploded.

The sky turned white. The stones rang like bells. Akea was flung backwards, screaming into the night, the bag flying from his shoulder. Excalibur shattered once more into a dozen glowing fragments, each tumbling across the ancient stone like angry gemstones.

Dialel, swinging like a very startled yo-yo, pulled himself back to the summit. He ran. Grabbed the green crystal.

And smashed it.

The world *shuddered*. A rip of sound tore from the bag, and suddenly, OFT and Geartrain popped back into the world at full size, blinking in confusion.

"Oooh," said Geartrain, "I really hate magic luggage."

The group reunited as the sky cleared. Storms fled. Colours returned to the sky. And Akea, wild and wounded, lunged at Hairspring to free Tetia —

And suddenly vanished with Tetia in a flash of remnants of crystal light.

Gone. For now.

Silence fell. The final rays of sun melted behind the horizon, drenching Stonehenge in firelit gold.

OFT dusted off his robe.

"Well," he said, "that was dramatic."

"They've escaped," Hairspring said, still breathless.

"Yes," OFT replied, "but so have you. And now the clocks are safe."

Geartrain raised a hand. "And... Christmas?"

Dialel smiled. "We can clear our names now?"

"No," said OFT. "You're still wanted fugitives." Then, at their horrified expressions, added, "Kidding! You're heroes. Time itself will tell your tale."

As the last golden light faded into stars and shadows, the three Cogletts stood, arms around each other, in the heart of Stonehenge. Victorious. Reunited.

And, at long last...

On time.

Epilogue: A Tick in Time Saves... Something

It had been a few weeks since the events at Stonehenge—weeks that, for most, passed with the dull clunk of calendar pages turning, but for Cogletts, ticked by with the gentle clickety-chime of cosmic satisfaction.

Dialel, Hairspring, and Geartrain had returned to London as heroes. Not the sort of heroes who wore capes or smouldered handsomely in the wind—though Geartrain had tried both and accidentally set fire to a lamppost—but true, celebrated, banner-hung-from-the-clocktower heroes. Their names were whispered in cuckoo clocks and sung by the kettle bells in every good horological household. Even the Big Ben bell gave an extra bong when they walked past. (Though that might've been indigestion from all the noise lately.)

Old Father Time, in his infinite (and sometimes frustrating) wisdom, had made sure everyone knew what the three had done. Not because he particularly liked fuss, but because the world needed to know what courage looked like when it came in three very small, occasionally squeaky packages.

They no longer worked at Shepton Gate, nor Big Ben, nor even the biscuit tin office beneath the Battersea Kitchen Clock. Instead, they were posted to a secret clock. So secret, in fact, that even the hands whispered as they moved, and the pendulum only swung when nobody was looking.

There, in a city where the pigeons wore sunglasses and even the shadows ran on time, they trained other Cogletts. Not in polishing or chime maintenance (though Geartrain still swore by a polish made of snail slime and hedgehog whiskers), but in survival. In strategy. In travel-by-human. (Which meant learning to operate underground turnstiles without being turned into jelly.)

They were preparing the next generation—arming them with knowledge, skill, and a firm understanding of how to bribe mythical beings like Jerry with cinnamon rolls.

Because, of course, threats weren't gone. Just... delayed. Like a particularly slow train, something else was approaching.

Akea and Tetia hadn't vanished. Oh no. They'd zipped through time and space using the Concordius Crystal, hurtling far away, to where even the world's most punctual sundial would lose track of them. But distance is nothing in the language of clocks. Time is round. And they were planning.

Plotting.

Ticking.

Somewhere in a volcano-circled land of forgotten hours, Akea was scribbling furiously into a leather-bound book with a pen made of fractured time. Tetia was watching something metallic rise from beneath the floor—something with gears that spun with monotonous, relentless precision.

And back in London, in a quiet corner of the Coglett's shared flat, Geartrain had solved his Rubik's Cube. Not through brilliance, but by rearranging the coloured stickers with a glue stick and a guilty smile.

"Finally," he whispered. "Now... what's a Metronome?"

Dialel looked up from a map. Hairspring looked out the window.

And somewhere, just faintly, the sound of ticking got... slower.

No. Not slower. Steady.

And steady, sometimes, is worse.

To be continued... in *The Monotonous Metronome*.

Printed in Great Britain
by Amazon